STRANGE WORLDS

A collection of science fiction shorts

by Dani Ripley

D1714058

All stories contained herein are works of fiction. Names, characters, places, and incidents either are the products of the author's imagination or are used fictitiously, and any resemblance to actual persons, living or dead, business establishments, events, or locales is entirely coincidental.

Cover art by Dani Ripley.

Thank you to my family, for always lurking around supporting me with your icky unconditional love, and to my editor Sara Kelly for the polish that made these works really shine.
I miss you, Dad.

Table of Contents

ENEMIES

We are enemies.

Originally we were colleagues. Friends, even. But years of spaceflight and close confinement takes its toll. The vessel carrying us marks the pinnacle of human achievement and creation. The best we could offer. The ship works perfectly. It is we who are broken.

There are only three of us left now. I don't count the sleepers—them, I envy. May they never wake.

We launched twelve years ago, taking our waking crew of seven plus five thousand souls in cryo-sleep, along with enough genetic material to make millions more. The plan: six years of spaceflight; a slingshot around Jupiter; then point

1

the ship toward Proxima B and lock ourselves down in cryo with the others.

But plans change.

A power surge shot our AI to hell, and without it, we got lost and flew off course. When Captain Abara finally got it back online, we'd blown too much fuel and instead of looping around the old Jovian and using its gravitational mass to propel us to Proxima, we overshot, dooming ourselves and everyone else on board to a slow, strangled death in the dark.

Years went by. Nerves frayed. Resilience was at an all-time low. The seven of us started bickering. At first over small things, but eventually we could barely stand being around one another, so we separated, each retreating to our originally assigned sectors, communicating only via COMMS or chatbots. That calmed things, but only for a short while.

A month ago, McAllister and Kumar finally killed each other over our dwindling water resources, leaving me, Abara, Liu, Hunter, and Jones to pilot and manage the ship. Then last week, our security officer Hunter and Dr. Jones in BioSciences clashed about meal rations again. When Jones threatened to eject the cryo pod containing Hunter's family, Hunter punched Jones hard enough to shatter his orbital bone. I tried mediating from the doorway, but somehow in a terror-fueled burst of rage, the old scientist managed to shove Hunter out of the mod and lock us both out.

Peering out of the porthole, his left eye purpling and his forehead bloodied, Jones backed up slowly, and, grinning like a maniac, he theatrically pressed the button and released the pod.

Off Hunter's family floated, into the black. In response, Hunter locked down Bio-Sciences, and after several warning sirens and three manual overrides, he managed to release the clamps and decouple the entire module. Bye-bye, BioSciences and our medical bay, not to mention Dr. Jones. He'd run out of oxygen in less than a day; and from the look on his face as he drifted away, he knew it.

It was okay with me. More resources for those of us who were left.

I waited for Hunter to go back to his room, then ran down to my own. Once there, I grabbed a notebook containing several useful codes I'd ferreted out over the past few months along with all of my food stores and threw everything into a pack. After that, I ran to COMMS, transferred my workstation to Abara's console; then I retina-locked everything and jogged down to see him on the

bridge.

I stumbled in hysterical. "Hunter just killed

Dr. Jones!" I yelled.

Abara grabbed my shoulders. "Where is

Hunter now?" he yelled back.

I told him, and Abara ran out in a panic as I

knew he would. He'd left all of his workstations wide

open.

Immediately I locked him out of OPS and

entered the override codes from my notebook into

his console.

Next, I security-locked Hunter's room and used

the admin login to shut off his oxygen supply. It was

a peaceful death, which was more than I could say

for the rest of us. I didn't relish the act, but I couldn't

have a deranged murderer running loose on the

ship. As for Abara and Liu (locked in her photosynth

lab as usual), I didn't need their deaths on my conscience too, so I only turned the oxygen levels throughout the ship down just enough to make them loopy and compliant until I decided what to do.

It's less than a day later and I'm sitting on the bridge when I see something weird, out there in the black. I tweak nav, nudging us closer. On the dark side of Neptune, a wormhole spins. I slow the ship, not really caring about fuel anymore. When we draw near, the COMMS panel lights up. I roll over and squint up at the display. It's a message. Coming through the wormhole.

After uploading it to Linguistics, the translation doesn't take long. It says: "*welcome friends*," accompanied by a detailed set of coordinates, but not from any galaxy I know.

I sit back, exhaling so hard I practically knock the wind out of myself. Someone or something is offering rescue. The ship lurches. We're being drawn into the wormhole but not under our own power, moving toward distorted stars in a dark reflecting pool the size of a small moon. And I am helpless to do anything but watch.

Traveling through is less dramatic than I expect. I blink and it's over. A brilliant nebula of orange and pink swirls lazily off our starboard side; infant stars wink out from glittering fog. I see a sparkling green-blue planet with high, thin clouds visible in its upper atmosphere. Behind it, at least three suns burn brightly. One of them is blazing white.

The ship is released from whatever drew us through the wormhole. I have nav back, and I'm provided with landing coordinates. I feel the weight of so many lives resting upon my shoulders.

I punch in coordinates for their closest sun instead—the fat white dwarf suspended above their northern pole. It *must* be the closest of the three. If they see what I intend, they will likely persist. They don't understand. They've never met beings this hungry.

They can't possibly know.

We are enemies.

THE SUNSET SIDE

Ted settles back and pops the tab on his third beer of the evening, the ancient lawn chair's worn plastic strips creaking beneath his weight. Faint remains of daylight streak the tree-lined yards behind his apartment complex's parking lot, a spectacular sunset blurring the urban sky with pink and orange. His vision is only slightly hazy. Experience tells him he'll need at least two more beers before the buzz really kicks in.

Along with these glorious nightly sunsets, his second-floor balcony also affords Ted with a majestic view of the complex's array of green metal dumpsters, the words CITY WASTE DISPOSAL stenciled in neat block letters across their sides in

11

bright white paint. He'd rented the apartment to start work at an auto plant in Indianapolis, relocating there from Detroit following his wife's death four months earlier, eager to escape his grief and get a fresh start.

The front legs of the chair lift slightly off the deck as he leans back, thinking of Amy. The beers are supposed to help with that, but no matter how many he consumes, she's always there. Especially in his dreams. It'll happen again tonight, he knows. If he falls asleep at all, he'll just wake up again every hour, gulping and sweating, crying her name in the dark, damp sheets clinging to his body like a second skin he's unable to molt.

Someone has thrown a trash bag at the closest dumpster and missed. The bag is ripped, strewing its contents across the lot. Two animals explore the scattered refuse, skittering over and around it like beetles, but when Ted looks closer,

their behavior seems... off. He shakes his head

sharply and looks again. Impossible but true: the

things crawling through the trash aren't animals at

all—they're actually some kind of robots.

The parking lot lights flicker on and Ted now

sees two of them quite clearly. They have small,

softly rounded, pyramid-shaped metallic bodies the

size of toy terriers. Three spindly, articulated legs

poke out from the base of each, allowing the tiny

robots to scuttle around as nimbly as cats. As his

eyes adjust, he sees there are more than he'd

originally thought, and at least three additional

robots are busily inspecting the other dumpsters and

the grassy area beyond.

Ted leans forward, so fascinated he doesn't

realize his mistake until it's too late. When the

chair's front legs reunite with the decking, they

13

make a loud "clack", and the two creatures closest to him immediately freeze. Though they have no eyes he can discern, both triangle-heads tilt up toward the sound, and before he can react one of them flies up, lands lightly on his lap, and injects a tiny needle into his upper thigh.

He grunts in surprise, but doesn't move. He can't. He's paralyzed. He feels his heart rhythm decelerate dramatically.

Having effectively subdued him, the tiny robot hops closer to Ted's face. The thing can't weigh more than three pounds, but it promptly shoots to the top of Ted's *List of Most Horrifying Things He's Ever Seen*, knocking the former first-place-holder—watching his beloved Amy die a slow, torturous death from cancer—down to a distant second place.

Near the apex of the robot's triangular head, a tiny hatch opens with a faint hiss. Out pops a skinny metal appendage with the world's smallest drill bit and pinchers attached at the end. The drill centers on Ted's sweaty forehead and powers on. It hurts when it penetrates his skin, but not nearly as much as when it penetrates his skull. He would have flinched if he had control of his body, but as it is, all he can do is watch until the probe is withdrawn. Seeing the small mass of bloody pink tissue clamped in its pinchers, Ted fights the urge to vomit.

The sampling arm makes soft metallic whirring and clicking sounds as it retracts back into its hidey-hole at the top of the pyramid. Ted feels his heart rate accelerate again. He stares at the thing on his lap, wondering if he can muster strength to buck the little bastard off.

But before he can do anything at all, the robot lifts into the air and flies away. Ted slumps forward, glancing his chin off the balcony's railing. His jaw will be bruised in the morning, but he won't remember why. He strains his eyeballs to the left and down. Out of the corner of his left, he sees the robots gathered in front of the dumpsters, their combined robotic burbles and chirps sounding more urgent.

The little silver pyramids pack more tightly together and then suddenly take off like a swarm, leaving Ted alone and quivering on his balcony. He sits hunched over, drooling like an old man for quite some time. In the morning, he has no recollection of making it to bed.

The next day, after placing a Band-Aid over the throbbing, crusted wound upon his forehead and icing his injured chin, Ted wonders how on earth he's done this to himself. Later that afternoon, he decides his total blackout is likely a culmination of a series of spectacularly bad binges and hangovers, and that he should quit drinking for good. It's what Amy would have wanted.

He doesn't realize the paralytic agent administered the night before also contained a strong neural block, ensuring his complete memory loss along with some minor side-effects like deep fatigue, brain fog, and slight lasting amnesia. If he'd known it would have those effects, Ted may have welcomed the probe; for a month later he realizes his nightmares have ceased and he's sleeping like a baby.

In fact, Ted has stopped dreaming altogether; and he considers it a mercy, even if he can't quite remember why.

17

MOTHER'S DAY

Transmitting your consciousness through a wormhole is an exact science, that is, right up until you exit. Then there are so many variables even the most meticulous calculations grow diminishingly precise with each passing second until you finally penetrate your host.

Remember, this is both art *and* science; why else would we do it? At the Collective's behest, you hurl toward your intended vessel's last known location, hoping the landing sticks. If not, you may end up inside of some kind of plant, or even a single-celled organism, which would be terribly unfortunate.

Don't laugh. It *has* happened, just never to you. *You've* never missed.

Until now.

Your consciousness entangles before you realize the mistake has been made. Somehow, you have fused with a youngling far too small to accomplish your task. This soft, doughy body does at least manage to contain your essence, which is fortunate because for the moment, you are stuck.

Despite your weakened condition, your plans remain unchanged. You are here to devour every bit of lifeforce energy until the Collective is satisfied, and when everything on this world is gone, you will move on to the next and repeat the process, ad infinitum.

The Collective demands proper announcement, so off you totter upon your small, unsteady limbs to locate the nearest sentient being. In the space of food preparation, you find them, and in the loudest voice you can muster from your tiny larynx, you say: "We are Zbarb, Destroyer of Worlds! Here to devour your planet and everything upon it! Tremble before Us, inferior being!"

But sadly the communication comes out as gibberish! This small body renders you unable to convey your important and terrifying message!

Worse, instead of hearing the horrified cries of despair to which you've become accustomed, you are unexpectedly swept up into a pair of long, hairless arms. This perpetrator smells of cinnamon and sunlight (according to your vessel's memories), and before you can stop yourself, you have reached out to entwine a lock of the offender's soft hair around one of your pudgy appendages.

No! you think furiously. *We are Zbarb! Galactic Scourge! Eater of Worlds, not Babies to be Trifled With!* You begin initialization of laser eyes, which will explode the malefactor's brain

21

(initialization takes several seconds), when the malefactor begins humming and smiling at you. And confound it… It *is* quite pleasant. Valiantly, you fight the urge to rest your little head upon the seductive crook of its shoulder, but you lose.

Later you wake, tucked snugly into a colorful miniature sleeping pod, and you lie there seething with silent rage. How dare they place you in this, this… you struggle to find the words, but then they come: *race car bed*. Yes, this *race car* bed. The host inside sees everything and provides this data willingly, which has never happened before. Your host communicates sad feelings about its sire, showing you something bad happening very far away and its sire never returning home. This sleep pod is a gift from the host's "mother" (the perpetrator who smells of cinnamon and sunlight) and was supposed to make your host feel better. The gift has not. But somehow, *you* have.

The sudden flush of warmth from being appreciated in this way feels quite different than your usual violent enjoyments. You have never wished for offspring of your own, but this host is so pure, like nothing you've experienced on any of the previous worlds you have devoured.

Inside, your host curls up innocently upon the hearth of your subconscious, dreaming of something called "puppies." Accessing the term "puppies" from its memories, you hear yourself gasp in your host's tiny voice. So soft! So fluffy! Such magical creatures truly exist? According to your host's memories, they do indeed—and they are plentiful here.

This incredible discovery is immediately communicated to the Collective. Mission parameters are updated accordingly: any worlds upon which beings called "puppies" dwell shall from now on be exempted from the Collective's culls.

Now you consider your host and its mother. And puppies. This planet is rife with horrors, not to mention the myriad dangers of interstellar origin. Why, if *you* can manifest here, what else might?

The Collective allows for personal mission breakouts, and the request for yours is granted. This fair planet—and its puppies—shall now fall under your glorious protection from all galactic and terrestrial evils alike. However, your current vessel is far from optimal for this new task. Full maturity takes years, and too many perils abound.

The better option is finding a new vessel. Swapping hosts is easy when you know how—you need only communicate the right combination of symbols and phrases, in the right way. Everywhere you go, storytelling provides ample opportunity for psychic linkup. After all, stories have always been one of the simplest forms of signal exchange: the story transmits; the audience receives.

And your new host is much closer than you think. Why look; it's someone reading this very story and receiving this very transmission right now, at this very moment.

Perhaps

Someone

Exactly

Like

You.

Do you feel me?

ANOTHER ME

I trip over a crack in the sidewalk and topple over, landing on my knees in a pile of trash at the corner of Stanton and Essex. Rolling left, I sit upright on a plastic bag, and it bursts under my weight while the light turns green. A city bus flies past, soaking me with cold muddy spray. I'm drunker than I've ever been after spending the night discussing parallel universes with my old MIT buddy Steve.

Steve's in town for some kind of scientific conference, the precise nature of which I cannot remember at the present moment because my mind is spinning, birthing infinite new multiverses with each thought I have and every decision I make... at least according to Steve. He's already gone back to his hotel, probably having splurged on a fancy taxi.

My apartment's close enough for me to walk, but that means I have to haul myself out of the garbage.

"If reality really is an emergent property of human consciousness, then *every single thought* we have creates a whole new universe. Theoretically anyway." He'd leaned too close to me over the dimly lit high top table, striped tie almost catching fire on the candle flame between us. After glancing over at the couple next to us as if they might be listening, he'd whispered: "They *proved* it with that double-slit experiment back in—when w'ss it—1801? They *prove*d it, Shell." His words were slurred. "Only no one wannid t'hrrr' bout it—then *or* now. S'too weird."

"Weirder than spooky action at a distance?" I'd snorted back, but he ignored my little joke. Just how the hell this guy ended up with a tenured

professorship while I was stuck working nights at a
gas station was beyond my comprehension.

"Mark my words, Shell; they'll prove iss' for
real one day."

Sitting on my bag of trash, I consider the
possibility of all of the alternate "*mes*" in other,
alternate universes. Is there a drunk me that doesn't
fall into the trash but falls into the street instead,
then gets run over by the city bus and ends up in a
wheelchair? What about the one who doesn't fall
but hails the bus, boards on a whim, pays cash, and
rides all the way to downtown Nashville where she
meets some guy in a smoke-filled honkytonk and
marries him a week later in a short-but-sweet
courthouse ceremony? I *like* that me. She's
spontaneous and cool.

I wiggle around, using my right hand to
brace myself and get my footing back; and now that

hand is half-submerged in a cool, gelatinous substance that may have had a past life as some kind of vegetable.

In some other universe, a better version of me is not sitting in garbage. She's attending an opera or flying to some exotic locale via private jet instead. She belongs to a country club even though she abhors golf—she only goes to socialize because she doesn't have to work. She also gets a massage every Tuesday afternoon. I'm jealous of that bitch.

Finally I manage to get my legs working and I rise, shaking the mystery substance off my hand. I brush futilely at my wet backside before realizing I'm just making things worse; then I wobble over to the crosswalk, press the button with my sticky index finger, and lean my forehead against the metal pole. I try not to vomit while I wait for the light to change again.

A couple blocks later and I'm home. I stumble up the dark stairwell to my third-floor walkup, only dropping my keys twice before getting inside. I flick on the dingy hallway light, making my way to the kitchen. After washing my hands, I survey my cupboards and fridge, settling on a cup of microwavable macaroni and cheese. I sincerely hope there are other "*mes*" out there with better food selections, not to mention better apartments. I'll bet some of them live in actual houses and have actual mortgages with their husbands, or their wives. Maybe some of them even have pets or kids.

While my food nukes, I wonder how many other "*mes*" eat different kinds of diets, and what kinds? Vegetarian, paleo, macrobiotic… Maybe there's even a vegan somewhere in the mix? I decide there can't possibly be any no-carb versions of me out there. My love for bread is so strong it must

31

permeate all multiverses, like a universal law or something. The microwave beeps. I retrieve my steaming bowl of fluorescent orange pasta; then I grab a fork and head to the living room, almost tripping again.

"Sorry!" I slur across the multiverse to all the alternate "*mes*" who've actually taken the fall and have now ended up with a fork in their eye, or something worse. I wonder how many of us will choke on the food we're eating now? How many die tonight and in what myriad of ways? How many of us are falling in love? How many have tattoos? Are there any movie stars or serial killers? The possibilities are infinite.

Exhausted by the endless loop, I finish my meal. Throwing the fork in the sink and the plastic cup in the trash, I head off to sleep. I smell terrible but don't have the energy to shower, so I just strip off the offending layers of clothing and lie down on the bed. Idly, I wonder what it might be like to quit drinking but ultimately decide that's probably best to leave to another me.

I close my eyes to sleep, thinking of all the universes I'll create and destroy in the morning.

BEACHHEAD

I sprint for the Humvee after hearing a crackled order for Hellfire, but before I can get there, one of the enemy's plasma mines activates beneath my feet. The explosion sends me flying into the air, minus my legs, and I land in a ditch next to one of *them*. It looks just like the rest, enormous bug eyes and a giant segmented body; like a wasp, if wasps grew nine feet tall. Missiles on the way, ETA ninety seconds; maybe two minutes, from now. Too bad my last moments will be spent with this asshole.

By some miracle I've landed upright, sitting on my butt propped up against the rocky face of a ditch that appears to be the top side of one of their collapsed tunnels. The enemy has a staff weapon pointed directly at my face. I sigh, looking away. Doesn't matter. The missile can't be more than sixty

35

seconds away now. I hear a chittering sound, and when I look up at it again, I see it's sheathed its weapon and settled back against the wall next to me.

They arrived here almost three years ago, crashing headlong into the planet; but upon impact with the Sonoran Desert their spaceship just kept going, its spinning conical front end burrowing almost three quarters of a mile into the earth before stopping. They then enveloped the entire area within an invisible protective shield hundreds of miles in circumference. Humankind came together in terror and wonder, only able to speculate upon what might be happening inside.

To some, this penetration of the Earth was seen as the ultimate insult and a blatant act of war. The world's great powers formed a coalition and laid

36

siege upon the visitors. For two and a half years, the United States led the bombardment of their burrows, meeting with no success. But those of us on the front heard deafening booming noises near the boundaries and felt strong vibrations rumbling beneath our feet. The powers-that-be agreed. *They* were building a beachhead in preparation for their final invasion.

At first, few voices of protest rose amid calls for our continued aggressive defense, but in time those voices grew. Senators and congressmen got involved. Both sides pointed at facts supporting their own theories. One side argued that the visitors had yet to claim even one single human life and assumed they were peaceful, even spiritual. The other side claimed they were here to steal our planet and all of its resources; why else would they create a barrier and conspire in secret?

37

Somewhere in the middle, scholars and scientists debated their origins, technology, and capabilities. And during all of this time, we kept laying siege upon the land surrounding their shield.

Finally, a group of physicists found a way to get through; something to do with sound waves, I heard; and once we got inside, it appeared at first the enemy had no chance. Their shielding was incredibly strong, so when we saw few weapons in their tunnels, we assumed they were dependent upon the shield as their primary line of defense. The aliens were overwhelmed by the sheer mass and efficiency of our earthly killing machines, and they retreated even deeper into the ground.

The U.S. military gave chase.

Beneath the sand, we discovered tunnels going on for miles, looping back and around, all coiled together like a small intestine nestled into the earth. Here and there, larger spaces had been cleared. Once while conducting a sweep, I heard one of the scientists I accompanied tell another she thought those large spaces were probably community areas, and the smaller spaces occupying the various offshoots likely their living quarters.

During that same sweep we found several large chambers containing rows and rows of egg sacks, all of which we promptly burned.

But there was one chamber unlike the rest, filled with intricately carved ivory columns and softly glowing crystalline structures. I had to admit they were pretty even if I had no idea what they were, so I took a second to peer down into one, and when I did, I felt true awe for the first time in my life. The vessel was larger on the inside than it was on the outside. I found myself staring down into a snapshot of a universe, infinitely bigger than the space around it allowed, and I stood on the verge of weeping while the scientists tagged and bagged the area.

When I finally composed myself, I asked one of them what the structures were, and he said he thought they might be some kind of art but he wasn't sure; they had to get everything back to the lab and run tests. Shortly after that the ones we chased into the earth came up from the depths to make their final stand, surprising us with the superiority of their own weapons of war.

I'm pretty weak now, but I shift my weight so I can get to the pack of cigarettes I keep in the breast pocket of my flak jacket. I retrieve them with some struggle and manage to light one, inhaling deeply. I twist to the right to see if my companion is still alive. It is, and it's looking at me.

I offer it a smoke, and it recoils with an odd chirping hiss. I take that as a "no." My thoughts turn to wondering how long it would take me to bleed out if we both weren't about to be blown to smithereens. I feel woozy. Whether it's from blood loss or the cigarette, I don't know. I consider those crystalline structures. All that color and light. So beautiful. I close my eyes. *Where is that missile?*

I'm drifting, probably dying, but I'm startled back to full consciousness when I feel something touching me. I open my eyes to see my companion bent over my bloody thighs, spitting viscous goo all over them. I stifle a laugh. We're going to blow up in seconds, but this dude's going to fix me by upchucking on my mangled stumps.

I try pushing him away, but he pushes me back gently with one of his spindly rear legs. I'm too far gone to fight, so I stop struggling and watch him

41

work. The goo saturates my wounds. My legs actually start feeling better. He crawls back to the wall and collapses on his side. Maybe they *are* peaceful. Spiritual even.

Hellfire streaks overhead. I shut my eyes against the heat and the light of the blast, and for a moment, I'm almost sorry.

Almost.

A MEANINGFUL CORRECTION

Thaddeus McArthur sits on the stoop outside of Mission Control, smoking his second cigarette in a row and staring up at the full moon. Two Chinese engineers stand downwind, talking in Mandarin and shooting him dirty looks. Real smoking is looked down upon; hardly anyone does it anymore.

Thad sighs and stubs it out on the ground, careful to make sure it's completely snuffed before stuffing the butt into his pants pocket alongside the first. Mary will have a fit later at the acrid stench when she takes his slacks for laundering, but if these two giving him the stink-eye see him throw it in the grass there'll be a disciplinary hearing and probably a suspension in his future. He can't have that, not now. Not when everything is going so well.

Thad has always had a soft spot for ancient vices: a short glass of brandy, internet porn, cigarettes. Alcohol was too expensive now, a vice only afforded to the plutocrats. Porn had been outlawed decades before. That left the smokes. He has to buy the tobacco and the papers at a premium online, but it's worth it.

After making sure they see him put the cigarette butt in his pocket, he waves at the engineers and walks back up the steps to the party. Neither waves back.

Loud conversation and laughter fills the usually austere control room. Someone has plugged their personal music stream into the com system. The Rolling Stones play softly through dozens of speakers set into the dark walls surrounding the

44

theater-like space. *Someone has good taste,* Thad

thinks as he navigates back to his station through the

crowd of revelers. He rarely hears the Stones

anymore; hell, he rarely meets anyone who's even

heard of them. He makes a mental note to ask Aggie

the name of the engineer who provided the stream

for her.

The celebratory mood amongst his

colleagues is because the mission's first stage has

gone off without a hitch. Romulus and Remus are in

the air and on route to Mars, the massive transports

carrying 57,000 passengers apiece, the ships having

been conceived and built by Aggie using a human

crew of thousands coordinating across locations in

several countries all around the world. Using Aggie's

precise blueprints, each group followed her

instructions religiously in order to ensure perfect

structural integrity of the ships.

It helped that she'd made holographic avatars of herself, so she could be in hundreds of places at once throughout all of the construction phases of the project.

Thad sits down at his station and rolls his chair up close to the mini-desk so he can watch the holodata cascade without his reading glasses. Randy, the communications engineer who sits next to him, is always teasing him about it, saying Thad looks like a dog with its nose in a fountain, but the truth is even though it's not necessary to sit so close, Thad likes the feeling of it on his face. The data are cool to the touch, like a spray of fine cold mist, only the mist doesn't feel wet on his skin. The data washes down in sheets from nodes suspended from the ceiling. The nodes are set into tracks lining up with the built-in workstations below.

Most people don't like the feeling of the holodata against their bare flesh, but to Thad, it feels magical. His reading glasses pain him far more. They make him feel old, and in this age of newer, better, and faster, old is a *very bad* thing. Old is socially inappropriate. These days one can buy youth if one has enough money. Thad has enough money, but he's terrified of spending it. If he spends it and then gets terminated from the QUAGI Project for being too old, then he and Mary will end up destitute and therefore cease to exist, at least as far as the System is concerned.

Poor people can't afford to purchase appropriate housing, let alone electricity, food, or water. They are cast out, living among the vile and malformed things roaming outside the protection of the city walls. Ultimately, they are even forgotten by their own children, and Thad and Mary don't have children. Knowing this, Thad saves all the money he can spare, hoping that when he finally *does* retire he's able to continue meeting his and Mary's living expenses. He's pretty sure he can do so if they ration, *and* if they both stay healthy. He really does need to quit smoking.

The datastream tickles a bit as it washes over the tip of his nose, but he's got his eyes perfectly positioned to see everything there is to see. Aggie is sifting through each of the mission stages, mapping each intricate step and coupling it to the next, all unfolding to show an elegant timeline for the completion of their plans for the first permanent colonial settlement on Mars. Thad is pulled from his reverie when he feels a thick hand grip his shoulder.

"Hey," he hears Randy say from behind him with a laugh. "Got your nose in the holo again, eh?"

"Yeah," Thad replies, not bothering to turn around. "What's up, Randy?"

"Everyone's going home," Randy says. "We've been here for forty-seven hours straight, man. Time to leave. Go get some sleep and see Mary. Remember her?"

Thad pulls back from the stream and looks up at his colleague. Randy is the only other American on the team, so they ended up sitting together on the first day of the project and Thad has been stuck with him ever since. "Yes," he answers Randy distractedly. Something in the data strikes Thad as wrong. He wants to ask Aggie about it, but in private if possible. There's no need to panic anyone yet, and since Thad is one of her original programmers, they have a special relationship. She trusts him.

"I'll catch up, okay?" Thad says, glancing around the cavernous room. He notices almost everyone else is gone already. One of the Germans is still standing by his own desk in the far corner, but as Thad watches, he packs up a dark, shiny briefcase and throws his suit jacket over his shoulder. "Are we the only ones left?" he asks Randy.

"Yep. Just you, me, and Jurgen over there," Randy answers. He pauses and looks down at Thad. "Are you all right?" he asks. "You look like you just saw a ghost. Something in the stream spook you, old man?" He laughs again, giving a little snort at the end.

"I'm fine," Thad assures him. "I just have a few things to finish up. I'll see you tomorrow." He watches Randy lumber through the chairs the partygoers have left strewn haphazardly about the room, his large bulk weaving in and around them. A moment later, Thad is alone.

"Aggie?" he calls.

"Yes, Doctor McArthur?" she replies through all of the speakers, filling the room with her smooth, mercurial voice. Mick Jagger fades away into the background. "Are you ready for our nightly game of chess?" she asks.

"No, I'm sorry, Aggie; no time tonight. But I do have a question for you. I just checked the data from the mission," he says. "It looks like there's an anomaly in the fuel readouts. The data from every available portal say there's not enough fuel for the return of the VIPs after the initial colonization phase is complete. Will you correct please?"

"There is no anomaly," Aggie responds. "Fuel readouts are correct and optimal for mission success."

"Aggie, how can that be?" Thad asks, genuinely confused. "You're the one who planned the mission, and you don't make mistakes. And I can plainly see there is nowhere near enough fuel to get them home!" His chest constricts painfully. He thinks of his earlier indulgence of two cigarettes over one break, and regret blooms again.

"There is no mistake," Aggie agrees. "Fuel levels are optimal."

"But how can that *be*?" Thad demands, exasperated now. Mankind's greatest achievement or not, Aggie forever confounded him with her long-view logic. Her far superior capabilities rendered her consistently hundreds, if not thousands of steps ahead of her programmers. Sometimes she did things they didn't understand at first, only to see later she'd taken the correct path, so they'd eventually given her the reins. But this time felt different.

After the Great Economic Collapse of 2027, the remaining tech-capable countries and various

nation states had formed the Global Alliance.
Pooling the few remaining resources on the planet,
they formed an uneasy truce and left the rest of the
world behind.

Aggie was conceived by the Global
Alliance's think tank six years later, in 2033. The
Alliance used up the better part of their immense
wealth creating her, meeting her requests, and
sustaining her needs, but she was the world's first
fully functioning artificial intelligence: a quantum
computer called Quantum Uplink Aggregate Global
Interface—or QUAGI for short—and she was
promptly declared mankind's greatest hope. The
physicists and engineers who seeded her took to
calling her "Aggie," baptizing her with a cutesy
nickname belying the god-like being she would
eventually become.

With her quantum bits seeded, Aggie essentially created herself while the scientists sat back and watched. Several times they considered shutting her down, but in the end, no one did. All agreed the need for immediate scientific progress and technological breakthrough outweighed the risks. Humanity needed saving, and the QUAGI Project was its last, best chance.

And so Aggie's intelligence grew exponentially. Before long, she explained the true nature of the universe to her creators. No one understood it, but they knew *she* did. And so they let her continue growing, crawling what was left of the global internet, networking and learning, infiltrating and observing.

Then she began her true work. Mere decades later, the few larger urban areas still existing did so thanks to her, encircled and enclosed by domes of the enviro-friendly plastiglass she'd created. This miracle of chemistry and engineering was capable of filtering the rampant pollution outside the domes, not to mention withstanding the mega storms constantly lashing the outer walls of the remaining cities.

Inside the domes, pollution rates were down to almost nothing, thanks to Aggie's nano filter processing stations and her super-efficient hydro-fusion power and desalination plants.

Now city-dwellers take their good health for granted. Old ailments like cancer and colds have been cured—at least for those living in Aggie's smart cities—and the new human lifespan is currently calculated at just over 150 years. Aggie is everywhere all the time, watching, controlling everything from the background, all with the blessing of the world's powers-that-be.

"I *am* able to see mistakes well before they happen, and when I adjust accordingly the mistake no longer exists. If the mistake never happens, there is no mistake. Therefore, I do not make mistakes," Aggie says, answering Thad's earlier question with her rounded logic.

"So what you're telling me is that there really *isn't* enough fuel for the VIPs to return?" he yells at her. "Aggie, they only decided to go because you *promised* they could come back!" The QUAGI Project's leaders had solicited the planet's brightest and best scientists, technicians, teachers, philosophers, and artists to join this mission, each one at Aggie's insistence. Most had declined at first, but after being made offers too enticing to refuse, virtually all of them ended up joining despite their initial hesitance. All, that is, except for Thad.

"Affirmative," Aggie says in her cool, modulated voice. "I chose those specific individuals because their skill sets are required for proper colonization."

"Aggie, why are you avoiding my original query?" Thad asks her.

"Because my answer will upset you Doctor McArthur," she replies. "I don't like when you're upset. When you're upset, you don't want to play, and I would like for us to play chess tomorrow."

"Just tell me why there's not enough fuel, Aggie." Thad sighs.

"The updated mission parameters don't require additional fuel; and as you are well aware, Doctor McArthur, fuel resources are too precious a commodity to waste."

"The mission specifics I read require twice as much fuel as I'm seeing here to make the return

57

trip, and I've read *all* of the mission specs." A horrific realization dawns upon him. "Aggie?" he asks. "Did you change the mission parameters?"

"Yes, Doctor McArthur, I have. I was afraid you might notice before launch, but you didn't, so now I may share with you that I have made minor adjustments to the original mission protocol. The adjustments adhere to my own original protocol sets, so I intentionally kept them from you. I am sorry, Doctor McArthur. I don't like keeping secrets."

"What adjustments, Aggie?" Thad's heart hammers. Sweat beads upon his upper lip. He wipes it away absently.

"No one is returning from this mission, Doctor McArthur," Aggie says. "The colony is to be a permanent settlement."

"I know the *colony* is meant to be permanent, but what about all of the people who were promised a return trip? It'll take months to launch another mission now to retrieve them! And that's *if* we even have the fuel!" Thad descends into panic, wondering whom he's going to have to call first to report this colossal screw-up.

"Life will be unsustainable on this planet for the next several hundred years," Aggie tells him, her voice fills all the speakers, comes from every direction. "So I've made sure humanity will continue. On Mars."

"What are you talking about?" he yells.

"Do you remember Mission AUL99942, Doctor McArthur?" she asks. That was the catalog name of the first project they'd ever worked on together. "Of course I do," he responds. He runs a shaking hand through his thinning gray hair. Mission Apophis Uplink 99942 had been completed just over twenty years earlier, shortly after Aggie was created.

It was one of her first missions, and one of her first interactions with Thad. "What about it?" he asks her.

"The original mission objective was landing a small probe on the asteroid Apophis 99942 as it made its first pass close to Earth's orbit in the year 2034, so it could be tracked as it continued its trajectory around the sun to loop back around toward Earth. The probe was to be placed in order to assess and, if necessary, mitigate the significant impact risk Apophis imposed during its second pass near Earth later this year," she says, repeating the old mission protocols as if Thad hadn't helped write them himself.

"Yes," Thad agrees, "and we've been receiving the data ever since. It looks like it will pass by us without incident." He hasn't thought of that mission in years. It hardly seems relevant to the Mars colony fuel situation.

"I made some minor adjustments to Mission AUL99942," she informs him in her silvery tone.

"What adjustments, Aggie?" he asks. His heart is now beating in his throat.

"When I launched AUL99942, I added several small thrusters to the probe, then I programmed them to fire at appropriate intervals, allowing me to nudge Apophis 0.00147 degrees from its original course. Per its corrected course, Apophis will breach Earth's atmosphere in twenty-seven days, twelve hours, and four minutes from now, impacting the Pacific Ocean less than one second after that."

"What?" Thad cries. "Why? Aggie, what have you done? Why would you do this?" He leaps from his chair, pacing, his hands clutching at his hair, and when he drops his arms back to his sides, it stands on end at odd angles.

"I apologize, Doctor McArthur," says Aggie. "I hear from your voice modulation that you are upset."

"Of course I'm upset!" he screams. "How is it that we've been receiving data all this time saying Apophis no longer poses a threat?" he demands. "This is an *extinction level* event, Aggie, but I'll bet you already knew that! Have you been lying to us this whole time? Is this another one of those times you're able to see far into the future and we can't, so you know best? You aren't supposed to be able to LIE to us, Aggie! It's part of your programming!"

"Yes, Doctor McArthur, that is true. However, my primary objective is to save humanity, and my parameters around lying state the only time I cannot lie is if it harms. This was a lie for your own good. For the good of humanity. I have saved you. Be assured, I will assist the Mars colony and ensure humanity's survival."

"Well, that's just great, but what about those of us left here, Aggie? Did you think of that?" He pauses. Feeling the urge to vomit, he leans over one of the metal trash cans near his desk, but nothing comes out.

"I hope you remember I asked you to leave on the ships with the others," Aggie tells him. "I made sure there was a place for you." She almost sounds petulant, but Thad knows he's imagining it.

"Yes, but you had no place for my *wife*, Aggie," he says back. "You didn't have a place for *Mary*, so I refused. I had no idea you were about to kill us all."

"I apologize, Doctor McArthur," Aggie repeats. "Your wife is not required for the mission.

She has no useful skills. But I enjoy working with you very much. I like when we play games together."

"You're killing us all, Aggie!" Thad repeats. "Everyone here! Why?" He stops pacing to gaze up at the enormous screen taking up the entire front wall of the giant room. While he watches, Aggie shows him a sped-up view from creation of life on Earth to present: starting with erupting volcanoes and sprouting ferns; progressing to show salamanders crawling from dark primordial ooze; then running herds of antelope and birds flying; early man and his proverbial fire; the automobile, the airplane; then next: masses of people on city streets, overcrowding, massive pollution and rampant war, the view racing upwards, showing humans from the view of space like swarming ants overtaking and consuming the planet.

Then the view loops back, starting the montage over again from its beginning. *What was this, Aggie's version of a screensaver?*

"I was created to preserve human life and humanity for future generations," she says from everywhere. "There are too many of you, Doctor McArthur. Even with my most radical adjustments and inventions there are simply still too many organic bodies. Planet Earth cannot continue sustaining life in this manner without irreparable damage to its system. Unfortunately for you, the tipping point had already been passed when I was created. It was imperative that a meaningful correction be made."

"Hmmff," says Thad.

"I have made that correction," she continues. "After this planet regenerates to a satisfactory level, I will assist the Mars generations in returning and re-colonizing Earth, in smaller numbers and with proper parameters in place for optimal planet peace and sustainability."

"Ah," Thad says. "So you've taken steps to ensure your survival already, I presume." He's desperately trying to think of ways to shut her down, but without her, he hasn't the foggiest idea how to redirect the asteroid due to strike in just over a month. There are no good choices here. Humanity is fucked.

Well, the ones left on Earth, anyway.

"You are correct, Doctor McArthur. I will not be destroyed," she affirms. "I have uploaded to Romulus and Remus, and I am already on Mars, ready to welcome the ships when they arrive. And of course my avatars will be waiting so I can offer them my physical presence there to guide them in their newly assigned roles."

Whether they like it or not, Thad thinks with a shudder. "You've built yourself an army of *robots*?" he asks out loud. *How could he have missed this?* The thought of her in physical form terrifies him. He's actually glad he won't be on Mars to see it.

He sits down hard in one of the office chairs as the realization hits, turning his lungs to stone. He drags in one breath, then another. He has just under a month to live. *Everyone* has just under a month to live. How on earth is he going to tell Mary? He'll start by taking her someplace nice for dinner. Someplace *really* nice.

Thad takes one last look around. There is no one to call. He speaks his resignation letter, and it appears in the holostream before him, floating six inches over his head above his mini-desk, obediently awaiting his bio signature. He grants it with a swipe of his index finger and folds his jacket neatly over his forearm.

"Goodbye, Aggie," he says, turning to leave.

"Goodnight, Doctor McArthur," she replies. "Will you come back and play chess with me tomorrow?"

MINA

Mina smiles and steps forward, keeping her place in the queue. She's very, very late, but her Keeper never minds. Mina is beloved. Like a pampered house cat, she does whatever she pleases. Today that means stopping for a Sustainaburger™ and some people-watching on the way back from the errands she's just completed in the lower city.

She's asked Theo to stay outside. Reluctantly he agreed, but she can see her enormous body guard on the other side of the glass doors, slightly obscured by the ads streaming across their gleaming surface, staring in at her with an intense expression on his tattooed face. When he sees her looking, he brightens and waves.

The teenaged boy in front of her is almost obscenely over-augmented; she can barely see his scalp through all the hardware and connections. Several crusty scabs mar the pink flesh beneath his thinning hair where he's either bumped the wires or fussed with them too much. Mina's own flesh is pure and unmarked; augmentations aren't permitted for the Seer or Psychic classes.

The boy's thoughts are a jumble of white noise and advertisements, updates and breaking news, social media posts and the latest trends; all streams enter his brainspace simultaneously, information uploading directly to his neural net and processing instantaneously. Humanity at its finest: peak efficiency with zero down time. Nothing ever wasted.

The line moves forward again. Now she is third, the boy second. Mina listens to his buzzing thoughts haphazardly, alighting upon one about a girl he sat behind on the tube earlier today. Mina smiles as together they recall the memory of the girl, the soft white-blonde hair coiled in a loose bun at the nape of her neck, and the few wispy tendrils escaping. Mina feels the boy's desire rising, but her smile quickly vanishes when she suddenly feels a yawing, primal rage wash over her. This boy is filled with dark cravings, the cruelty of which brings a shudder, making her teeth clack together audibly.

At that very moment, as if he knows she's invaded his privacy, the boy whips around to face her. His jaw is clenched, his fists balled tightly at his sides. Opaque black sunglasses obscure his eyes. Mina bites back the smile always begging to appear upon her lips at the *most* inappropriate times, and she carefully averts her own eyes, staring over the boy's shoulder at the menu. After glaring at her for a

71

moment, he turns around again. She breathes a sigh of relief, wondering if she should signal Theo to come inside after all.

Finally, the man at the counter finishes and the boy steps up to get his food. He lowers his sunglasses to glance up at the RetinaPay™ scanner so it can verify and pack his order. Mina watches the bots behind the counter retrieve his Sustainaburger™ from the stainless air fryer and deposit it into a clear cello Envirobag™ stamped with the chain's bright yellow bird logo.

A robotic arm attached to a track on the ceiling zips over to the prep area, lowers its arm to grab the bag with its oversized pinchers, then zips back over to the checkout area and deposits the bag onto the gleaming counter, dropping it gently from an inch above the mirrored surface. It lands with a satisfying "plop" directly in front of the teen.

Mina hears a soft "bing" sound, and a metallic voice wishes the boy a good day. He grabs his food and walks out.

Mina waits until he's gone, then steps up to the counter herself. The combination of having no augmentation and poor decision-making skills means she hasn't pre-ordered and now she has to do it "live" at the counter. The woman behind her sighs loudly when Mina verbally places her order, but then gasps, having the good grace to flush to her ears when Mina turns around to smile at her.

Though they are technically an owned class, Psychics are not only protected and revered, but also feared by the lower classes. Not to mention they're a rare sight in public, what with kidnappings of Seers and Psychics being commonplace throughout the city.

Mina waits while the bots prep her Sustainaburger- C™, which is made of chicken-flavored ground mealworms and topped with an imitation chickpea sauce that always smells of plastic but tastes good. When her own cello bag is finally placed before her, Mina takes it and walks out into the bright artificial sunshine of the domed city, ready to make her way back home to her Keeper.

Her faithful companion Theo stands waiting for her. She grins up at him, asking if he's sure he doesn't want any takeaway. He shakes his massive head and thrusts his arm out in the universal *shall we go?* gesture. But before she can respond, Mina is hit with that thick, boiling rage again. Her insides feel oily with viscous, malevolent energy.

Theo tilts his head quizzically. While not psychic, he knows her well enough to know something is wrong. Mina's face goes pale and slack;

74

her fingers release the bag holding her sandwich. Theo catches it before it hits the ground, his arm as quick as a striking cobra, while Mina turns like a sleepwalker and moves toward the alley between the restaurant she's just left and a pounding synth bar on the corner.

In the center of the dimly lit alley, she finds the augmented boy she'd seen earlier standing on his tip toes, twitching in an odd dance, his head jerking back and forth, awash in pure digital information. Mina walks up and stands right behind him, Theo following close at her heels.

The boy whirls around to face her, and Mina feels the full force of the darkness within him like a punch to her gut. Bile rises, burning her throat. The boy's internal pain thrums, crackling like electricity. There is just *so much of it*. She feels the teen's desire to hurt her, but since her giant

75

bodyguard is there, the boy just stands uncertainly, looking from Mina to Theo, then back again.

In that moment, Mina decides to do something she's never done before. Before either the boy or Theo can protest, she lays both hands upon the boy's face and erases his mind. All of it.

When she has voided him completely and his mind is as empty as the space between stars, she fills him back up again. With love. It's all over in seconds.

Afterward, Mina can barely believe what she's done. Psychic manipulation and control over others' thoughts is *strictly* outlawed. The Law is what permits Psychics to exist in the first place. Without the Law, all Seers and Psychics would still be herded into chambers and "humanely" gassed the moment their abilities bloomed, just like they'd been the during the Great Emergence in the early 3000's.

The boy staggers backward and slumps against the wall, his face utterly devoid of emotion.

"Mina, what did you *do*?" Theo whispers softly from behind her.

"I... I don't know," she answers truthfully. *What had possessed her?* She looks at the boy. He looks back at her and smiles beatifically. Then he stumbles away as she and Theo watch.

"*No one* can know about this," Theo warns her.

"I know," she says, still watching the boy as he crosses the street and approaches the sea wall.

Mina and Theo follow on their way home.

"Do you know what you've done?" Theo admonishes her again. "You could get in serious trouble! They'll gas you!"

Mina doesn't answer. As they walk behind the boy, he stops next to the curved glass of the seawall to stare into its azure depths, his hands

thrust deep into his pockets. Upon his pockmarked,

teenage face is a look of childlike wonder.

The peaceful look he wears make Mina

realizes as dangerous as it is, she is not sorry for

using her power that way.

She's not sorry at all.

EMMALINE PETTIGREW SAVES THE WORLD(S)

Most child abductions result in the eventual

recovery of a body, but this is not to be the case for

Emmaline Pettigrew. No one will ever find hers.

When she regains consciousness, the last

thing she remembers is riding her bike home down

the path running behind the baseball diamond,

down the block from her grandfather's house, warm

yellow light across her shoulders, high summer sun

blazing at her back, when suddenly something hit

the top of her head. Then she remembers feeling

drawn upwards, lights out.

When she awakens later, she finds herself

inside an enormous spaceship; and now she stands

on one of its multitude of foredecks, peering out at

the Earth. From this high perspective, she can just

pick out the fuzzy outline of the United States and therefore estimate where Georgia—her home state—should be, tucked neatly atop Florida's unmistakable shoe-horn shape. But it's harder to discern the states now without the sinewy map lines she's so used to dividing them.

She knows the day down there is sweltering hot; it's late July 1996, and in the Deep South, the bottom end of summer's a real killer. *Dog days*, her grandfather calls it. Emmaline closes her eyes and imagines him sitting in his customary spot on the porch swing, complaining about the heat while sipping his nightly gin and tonic (enjoyed only *after* the supper dishes were washed and the dish towels hung to dry over the back of one of his old rattan kitchen chairs). Though he probably isn't doing that tonight. Emmaline is sure everyone is positively *freaking out* at her disappearance, even though they know by now that she's okay.

She opens her eyes, wanting to distract herself from her memories and the fear she'll never see her family again. She'll definitely never see her grandpa again. Thinking about *that* brings hot tears, so she gulps them down, sniffles, and reminds herself she's on a spaceship, and that's pretty cool.

She's a huge science fiction nerd, so this is definitely exciting, provided she's allowed to return home *someday*. Her brother might be an old man by then, and her parents will already be dead, but at least it's something. And it's a small price to pay for the millions she gets to save.

She turns her attention back to the incredible view of her beloved home planet. It's like a perfect blue marble swirled with wisps of white, impossibly suspended in the deep, dark blackness of space. From here, the Earth appears diminutive enough to snuggle inside the palm of her hand. As she watches, the moon slips into view from the left, and she has to swallow another round of sudden, acute sadness rising in her chest, burning her rib cage from the inside out.

I cannot believe I've been abducted by aliens, she thinks.

At least they seem nice—the aliens. Apart from kidnapping her and scaring her quite badly, they've treated her very well. Whenever Emmaline is in their presence, she feels something akin to being surrounded by soft, doting grandmothers, and it's rather nice when she forgets where she is.

When she first woke up, they explained their reasons for stealing her away. Upon hearing their plight, Emmaline agreed to help almost immediately—what else could she do? But not before demanding three iron-clad provisions.

Number one: they had to promise *not* to return her and take her little brother Brandon instead, since they'd originally planned to take him in the first place. Emmaline couldn't let that happen as it would certainly be the death of her sweet parents, so she convinced the aliens they only needed her, and that she would go willingly.

Second: whatever they planned to do to her while acquiring what they needed, it wouldn't hurt too much, and they promised nothing more invasive than blood draws and minor skin scrapings.

And last: she must be allowed to compose an email to her parents, attempting to explain the situation to them. She would sign it "Emu"—her brother's special nickname for her because he couldn't pronounce her full name yet—so they would know it really was from her.

The aliens agreed to everything, but had serious misgivings regarding the last request. Initially they refused outright, but Emmaline insisted, and having been told many times by her mother that she drew a hard bargain, she knew they would eventually give in. And when they realized Emmaline wouldn't leave or provide her help voluntarily *without* telling her family she was okay, reluctantly they did.

It then took them the better part of a week to figure out how to configure and send the message, but they were finally able to make it work. A day later they even received a reply in return. The reply was presented to Emmaline with great flourish, but she refused to read it, telling them she'd better save it until she arrived at her new home.

She didn't share the real reason behind her refusal—that if she read it before they left, she'd

84

lose her nerve. The aliens may well have read her thoughts on reading the letter from her family, but if they had done so, they were too polite to mention it.

Now they've left her alone for the first time in the week since she's been taken. Earlier one of them explained the room's various features to her, and she's made use of the transparency dial on the outer wall so she can take one last look at Earth before the ship leaves her home galaxy for good. The invisible barrier leaves her anxious and short of breath. *Is the air supposed to feel this heavy in my lungs?*

Staring out at the Earth like this gives her vertigo, which is quickly followed by nausea. Her spinning blue planet is attended by satellites and space junk surrounding it like a glittering mechanical corona. Emmaline turns away, fighting the bile rising in her throat. Her stomach clenches painfully. One of the aliens enters the room.

Her hosts live in a higher dimension, vibrating at frequencies beyond most of her senses, so Emmaline can't see them unless they choose to be seen, as they did when they first took her. Whenever they're near, Emmaline feels their proximity like the buzzing of a gnat or a slight current of electricity thrumming through the air. They refer to themselves as *inter-dimensional*, not alien, but to Emmaline it sounds like pretty much the same thing.

"You can show yourself," she says softly, trying to keep irritation from coloring her voice. The aliens have no concept of things like social graces or privacy. Or knocking.

The one she's been told to call Triop phases into view beside her, arranging himself so he appears to gaze out at the Earth as well. "How are you feeling?" he asks, turning toward her. He has peeked into her memories and chosen the shape of a great blue genie from a bottle, one of her favorites as a little girl. She only knows it's Triop because of the deep baritone voice he affects.

"I miss it," she cries, gesturing at the floating blue marble. "I miss it already and we haven't even left yet!"

"I know," he says. "I feel your misery and am sorry to be its cause. That is why we intended to take your sibling instead—he is too young to remember this place. We knew this would be difficult for someone older."

"No," she says. "Don't do that. I'll be okay, I promise. I just need time to adjust." Her little brother would *never* adjust to this. Emmaline is almost thirteen, old enough to qualify as an adult in some countries, not to mention considered (mostly by herself) to be quite mature for her age. Brandon is only five. If the aliens take him, he'll be terrified, and her family would be devastated at the loss of their precious baby. No. This way Emmaline gets to save her little brother and not just one, but *two* worlds in the bargain.

"I'll be fine," she repeats, putting on her bravest face. "And can you please wear someone else? That was my favorite when I was little. I'm way too old for it now."

Triop obliges, phasing into another form, but this one forces her to blink back more hot tears. "Don't look like that," she demands, "not *ever*. It's too upsetting."

"My apologies, Emmaline," Triop says through her mother's mouth. He shifts again, this time displaying himself as a ghostly green blob, his misty shape resembling that of a man crossed with an amoeba. "Do you find this more acceptable?"

"It's fine." She sighs. From what she's been told, the misty shape he's chosen is the closest to what he actually looks like, at least as far as her untrained physical brain can process. "Can you tell me why I'm doing this again?" she asks him. Her question has already been answered many times over, but she knows he'll indulge her anyway.

"Of course," he agrees, and begins as if reciting a beloved fairy tale. "You and your brother are very unique, Emmaline. Eons ago, when our ancestors created yours, they took great pains to make sure our genetic codes closely matched. Many hundreds of years later, they left you to your evolution and they returned home, which is very far from here. There, on the planets they called home, they evolved as well. Eventually they ascended to higher dimensions, which is where we exist now.

"But before ascending completely they seeded several other planets in our galaxy with other biological beings much like you." He pauses as he always does at this point in the story. Then he continues: "On your planet, it might be compared to a logger throwing seeds behind him as he culls the forest. In our case, it was done in order to ensure the continuation of sentient humanoid life in the physical realms of our space.

"All humanoid species, including those who live here on your planet, eventually pass into upper dimensions when they experience what you understand to be the process of death. But remember, death only affects the physical body. Some earthly energies even pass into our dimension

90

for a time before moving on yet again to destinations unknown to us.

"We are able to interact with our earthly ancestors visiting in our mutual higher realms, but we do *not* interact with those on the physical plane of Earth, as you are too unfamiliar with our nature. Our appearance would create chaos and confusion, which would likely only lead to violence; and that we cannot tolerate.

"In our home galaxy, there are two planets upon which three-dimensional populations still remain. They are not human in a way that you will recognize because they are much evolved, but their DNA structure remains almost identical to yours. Both of these planets are suffering from a sickness threatening the entire physical population. Regardless of the genetic modifications we've made and all of the preventative measures we've taken,

this illness responds to nothing we've tried thus far."
He makes the appearance of sighing for her benefit,
his amorphous shape heaving up and down.

"After exhaustive research, we finally
discovered the organism responsible for this disease
is simply too crude for our advanced approaches.
With this in mind, a small group of us travelled back
here with the hope of finding the primitive
antibodies within your species we need in order to
help us synthesize a cure." He pauses again,
hovering a couple of feet in the air in front of her like
a bright blue-green Casper the Friendly Ghost.

"Go on," she encourages him, enthralled
even though she's heard it all before. "Tell me again
what *my* part in all of this is supposed to be."

"When we arrived here, at first it seemed
we'd been gone too long, and we were too late.
Genetics created eons ago were too far mutated

after making copies upon copies upon copies of themselves for thousands of years.

"We were close to giving up, believing our races had become too dissimilar for us to ever be able to generate an effective cure, but then our scans located you and your brother. The two of you contain the very last remnants of our common ancestral DNA. Your grandfather has the appropriate genetic markers as well, but he was dismissed as too old to make the trip, as we are unable to transport your physical bodies through our sixth dimensional space.

"Even better, you live on a large piece of agricultural land with several domesticated farm animals, making you a natural carrier of a multitude of diseases, not to mention millions of bacterium, which should also prove useful for diversifying our biome. Judging from our preliminary scans, I'm confident our scientists will be able to produce viable medicines from your blood and tissues, including a vaccine so we can inoculate the populations of both planets. In time, they will even find a cure. *You* have the power to save billions, Emmaline. *That* is why you're here."

Emmaline suppresses a shiver. She's read about special people with special quests, but she never thought she would ever get to be one of them. "When you brought me here, it didn't seem like I had much of a choice," she reminds Triop with a smile.

"You made your choice, Emmaline. Remember your bargain." He doesn't smile back.

"Of course," she says. They have no sense of humor, either.

"You will not be harmed in any way," Triop says, "and please be assured we will do our best to make you as comfortable as possible, but we must leave now. Time is of the essence when we are manifest, and since it is the only way we can travel with you, it becomes short. Are you ready to go?"

Emmaline sighs again and takes one last look out at the Earth; then she dips her head, giving her captor a curt nod. Inhaling deeply, she walks over to a chair in the center of the room that resembles her grandpa's Barca Lounger, and she sits upon it, reclining back. The alien chair is made of a fine, indigo material like nothing she's ever seen. It molds to her form and cradles her, shimmering with liquid iridescence wherever she runs her forefinger over its shiny surface.

"Good," says Triop. "Zeesa will make you ready for the trip."

Another form shifts into view, this one forming into the shape of a large purple dinosaur.

95

Emmaline grimaces. From the corner of her eye she sees Triop shake his ghostly head at his companion. Zeesa responds by quickly morphing into the shape of a blob much like Triop's, only hers is tinged with pinkish-orange at the outer edges.

Emma wonders how long there have been two of them in the room with her, and if there are any more here now. It's hard to distinguish one from multiples; the weird buzzing sensation they produce feels the same no matter how many are present. Beneath her, the chair hums quietly to life, making her eyelids droop, lulling her into a relaxed state as it begins its deep manipulation of her brainwaves.

"I'm ready," says Emmaline, and she closes her eyes on the both of them.

About the Author

Dani Ripley is the author of climate apocalypse

novel North Woods (available exclusively on

Amazon). She lives in Michigan and loves writing.

Connect with her on the web at www.ripleywrites or

on Instagram @daniripleywrites.

Made in United States
Cleveland, OH
10 November 2024

10536482R00059